This book belongs to:

....

....

....

Sam McBratney
There, There

ILLUSTRATED BY
Ivan Bates

B|F|&|F
BRUBAKER, FORD & FRIENDS
AN IMPRINT OF THE TEMPLAR COMPANY LIMITED

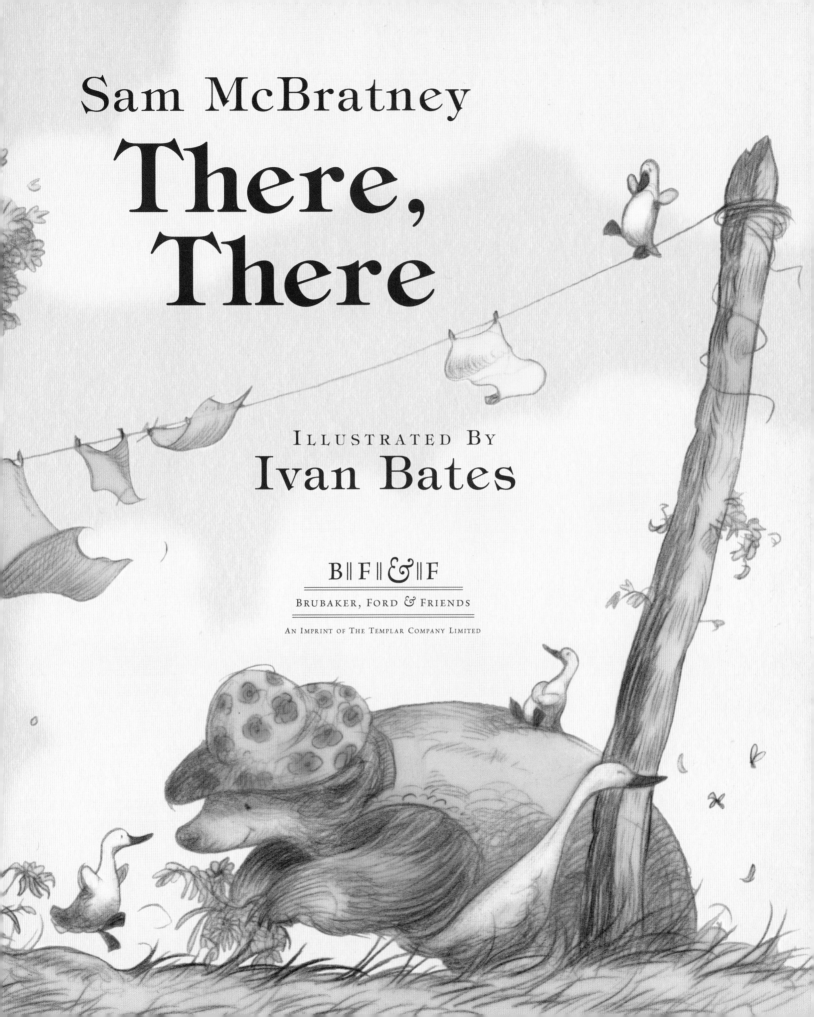

Little Hansie Bear,
who loved to pretend,
thought it would be fun
to walk like a duck.

Unfortunately he fell
over sideways into
a deep-down-ditch.
He hurt his knee and
couldn't get out again.

His dad came to help.

"What were you doing?" he asked.

"I was trying to walk like a duck!"

"Well that's not easy," said
    Hansie's dad, "unless you *are* a duck.
    Let's try a plaster on that knee."
    He gave Hansie a big hug.
    "There, there, it won't be sore
    for long, you'll see."

And he was right.
After a few minutes
and a few jumps,

just to be sure...
Hansie was ready
to play again.

His plan was to dig down deep
in the sandpit and dig his deepest
hole ever. But, it was a windy day
and all sorts of things went blowing
in the wind. Hansie got sand in his eyes,
and it really made them sting.

His dad, who was still close by,
picked him up for a cuddle.
"There, there," he said.
"Do blinkety-blink like this
and you'll soon be better."

Hansie blinked his eyes...
then a few more blinks
just to be sure...
and his eyes were as
good as ever.

Then some of
Hansie's friends
came to play
on his swing among
the trees...

but guess what!

Hansie bumped his
head on a branch, and
it was a hard bump.

Dad saw what happened.
"There, there, Hansie," he said.
"I'll give it a rub and
you'll be fine."

And he was right again.

Hansie Bear ran off
to play a game
of hide-and-seek
with his friends.

Later that same afternoon, when
the friends had all gone home,
Hansie saw his father coming
very slowly through the garden gate.

Hansie ran to meet him.

"I hurt my foot," said Dad. "I stepped
on a thorn, and my goodness it is sore!"

"Were you trying to walk like a duck?"

"I was *not* trying to walk like a duck."

Soon Mum came to see what was happening.
They made Dad sit on the garden seat.
"Ouch!" he said, as Mum pulled out the thorn.
"We are *definitely* not having a good day!"

This was like falling into the deep-down-ditch.
Or getting sand in your eyes.
Or bumping your head a hard bump.

"I know
a good thing to do!"
said Hansie…

And he gave his dad one
of his tightest ever hugs.
And then Hansie said,

"There, there, we'll be
all right now."

And so they were.

For Caroline
To mark a fine collaboration
—SMcB

For Rachel,
with love
—IB

A BRUBAKER, FORD & FRIENDS BOOK,
an imprint of The Templar Company Limited

First published in the UK simultaneously
in hardback and paperback in 2013 by
Templar Publishing,
Deepdene Lodge, Deepdene Avenue,
Dorking, Surrey, RH5 4AT, UK
www.templarco.co.uk

Text copyright © 2013 by Sam McBratney
Illustration copyright © 2013 by Ivan Bates

Designed by Amelia Edwards
Edited by Amy Ehrlich and Penny Worms

First edition

ISBN 978-1-84877-992-1 (hardback)
ISBN 978-1-84877-807-8 (paperback)

Printed in China